This book belongs to

_____

A READ-ALOUD STORYBOOK

Adapted by Catherine Hapka

Illustrated by the Disney Storybook Artists

Designed by Disney's Global Design Group

Random House 🏠 New York

EXPERIMENT 626

Far out in space, the Galactic Council was holding a trial. A scientist named Jumba was accused of creating a dangerous experiment.

Jumba admitted he *had* created something—a creature he called Experiment 626.

"He is bulletproof, fireproof, and can think faster than a supercomputer," Jumba said. "His only mission... *to destroy everything he touches! Ha ha ha ha ha!*"

3

The Grand Councilwoman sent Jumba to jail and told Captain Gantu to take Experiment 626 to a distant planet.

Gantu's ship hadn't gone far before Experiment 626 broke free.

"Red alert!" Gantu cried. "Fire on sight!"

But it was too late. Experiment 626 had escaped in a red police cruiser—and he was headed straight for Earth!

Experiment 626 was so dangerous that the Grand Councilwoman wanted to destroy the place where he landed.

But Agent Pleakley, who was an "expert" on planet Earth, stopped her. "Earth is a protected wildlife reserve," he explained. "We've been using it to rebuild the mosquito population."

So the councilwoman freed Jumba from jail and sent him and Pleakley to recapture Experiment 626.

Meanwhile, on a small Hawaiian island, a little girl named Lilo was supposed to wait outside her hula classroom for her big sister, Nani.

But when Nani arrived, Lilo was gone.

Nani ran home. When she got there, she looked through the doggie door and saw that Lilo was lying on the floor, listening to records. Nani tried the door, but it wouldn't budge. Lilo had nailed it shut.

"Lilo?" Nani called. "Open the door!" But Lilo wouldn't.

9

Nani and Lilo were orphans, so they lived by themselves. That day a social worker named Cobra Bubbles was coming to the house. If Nani seemed like a bad guardian, he could take Lilo to live with another family.

Cobra arrived to find Nani trying to pry the door open. He did not looked pleased at all. Nani had to climb through a window to let him into the house.

"Do you often leave your sister home alone?" Cobra asked as he stared at the stove. It was covered with pots overflowing with bubbling glop.

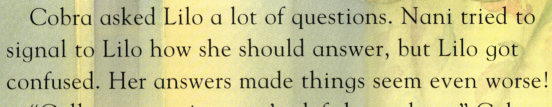

Cobra asked Lilo a lot of questions. Nani tried to signal to Lilo how she should answer, but Lilo got confused. Her answers made things seem even worse!

"Call me next time you're left here alone," Cobra told Lilo. Then he turned to Nani. "In case you're wondering, this did *not* go well," he said sternly. "You have three days to change my mind."

Nani was worried and upset. "Do you want to be taken away?" she asked Lilo angrily after Cobra left.

Later, Nani went to Lilo's room to apologize for getting angry.

"We're a broken family, aren't we?" Lilo asked sadly.

"Maybe a little." Nani gave her sister a hug and then tickled her. Lilo laughed.

The lights flickered, and Lilo looked out the window. "A falling star!" she cried. She shooed Nani out of her room so she could make a secret wish.

"I need someone to be my friend," Lilo whispered as she knelt by her bed.

Nani was listening in the hall. She felt sad that Lilo was lonely.

Not far away, Experiment 626 was crawling out of a smoldering crater. What Lilo saw hadn't been a falling star at all—it was the red police cruiser crashing to Earth!

LILO'S NEW FRIEND

Some truckers found Experiment 626. Thinking he was a dog, they took him to an animal shelter. The next day, Lilo and Nani went to that same shelter. Nani thought a dog might keep Lilo from feeling lonely.

Meanwhile, Experiment 626 was trying to escape. He crawled along the ceiling toward the shelter door. When he got outside, he saw Jumba and Pleakley waiting for him. He quickly crawled back inside.

Lilo walked into the kennel. All the cages looked empty. The animals were hiding from Experiment 626!

When he saw Lilo coming, the alien pulled in his extra legs, his antennae, and his back spikes. He figured that if he looked like a dog, the little girl might help him escape.

"Hi," Lilo said happily. He was the most interesting dog she'd ever seen!

Nani and the animal shelter woman were shocked when Lilo came out with her new friend.

"Does it have to be *this* dog?" Nani asked Lilo.

"Yes," Lilo said. "He's good, I can tell. His name is . . ." She thought for a moment. "Stitch."

Nani sighed and gave Lilo two dollars so she could buy Stitch.

Outside, Jumba and Pleakley were still waiting. They weren't allowed to hurt humans, so they could only watch in frustration as Stitch left with Lilo.

While Nani went to work, Lilo and Stitch took off on a wild ride around the island. But everywhere they went, Stitch seemed to get into trouble.

Later, Lilo and Stitch sat in the luau restaurant where Nani was a waitress and her friend David was a fire dancer.

Lilo drew a picture of Stitch. "This is you," she told him. "This is your badness level. It's unusually high for someone your size. We need to fix that."

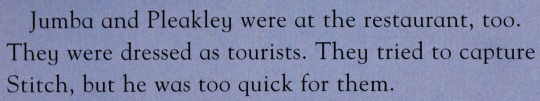

Jumba and Pleakley were at the restaurant, too. They were dressed as tourists. They tried to capture Stitch, but he was too quick for them.

When Stitch tried to swallow Pleakley's head, the restaurant manager came running over. "Nani, is that your dog?" he demanded. Then he fired her.

Nani wanted to take Stitch back to the animal shelter. Lilo couldn't believe her ears. "We adopted him! What about 'ohana? Dad said 'ohana means family. Family means nobody . . ."

". . . nobody gets left behind," Nani finished. With a sigh, she agreed that Stitch could stay—for now.

That night, Lilo showed Stitch the bed she had made for him. He liked hers better, though, so he crawled up onto it and grabbed her pillow. Beneath it was a photograph of Nani, Lilo, and their parents.

"Be careful of that!" Lilo cried, and grabbed the photo. Stitch saw that Lilo was upset.

After Lilo fell asleep, Stitch looked at her books. He found one called *The Ugly Duckling* and woke Lilo up to show it to her.

"He's sad because he's all alone," Lilo explained sleepily, pointing to the picture of the little duck.

The next day, Cobra Bubbles came back. "Heard you lost your job," he told Nani. Just then, Stitch appeared and threw a book at him.

Nani promised she would find a new job, and Lilo said she would teach Stitch to behave.

Nani went out looking for a job, but she didn't have much luck. Lilo didn't have much luck training Stitch, either.

Later, Nani and Lilo met David at the beach.
"We've been having a bad day," Lilo told him.
"Hey, I might not be a doctor," David said, "but I know that there's no better cure for a sour face than a couple of boards and some choice waves." Nani agreed—they would all go surfing!

Everyone had a great time—even Stitch, who hated water! But then Jumba appeared. He tried to capture Stitch by pulling him underwater. He almost pulled Lilo under, too, but Nani saved her. Stitch escaped from Jumba, but he couldn't swim! He began to sink to the bottom of the ocean.

David rescued Stitch. Everyone was okay, but Cobra Bubbles had seen Lilo get pulled underwater. "You need to think about what's best for Lilo," he told Nani, "even if it removes you from the picture."

"It's like they've been cursed or something," David told Stitch sadly.

Stitch realized he was pulling the little family apart.

That night, Nani thought about what Cobra had said. Maybe Lilo really would be better off without her. Nani held her little sister close and sang her a beautiful Hawaiian song.

Later, Lilo looked at the photo of her parents. "'*Ohana* means family," she told Stitch. "Family means nobody gets left behind." Lilo sighed. "But if you want to leave, you can."

Stitch knew that it would be best for Lilo if he left. He took *The Ugly Duckling*, climbed out the window, and disappeared into the night. He hoped he would find his own family.

NEW RULES

Early the next morning, Pleakley received a call on his intergalactic communicator. The Grand Councilwoman was not pleased to hear that Stitch had still not been captured. She fired Jumba and Pleakley.

"Now we do it *my* way!" Jumba told Pleakley happily.

The next morning, Lilo told Nani that Stitch was gone.

Just then David arrived. "Nani!" he cried. "I think I found you a job! But we have to hurry!"

Nani was excited. "Stay here for a few minutes," she told Lilo. "Lock the door and don't answer it for *anyone*, okay?"

Meanwhile, Jumba had found Stitch and was chasing him through the forest. Stitch headed for Lilo's house—with Jumba right behind him!

Stitch ran into Lilo's house.

"Ha!" Jumba cried, crashing into the house. "Hiding behind your little friend won't help."

Lilo grabbed the phone and made a call. "Hello, Cobra Bubbles?" she said with a gasp. "Aliens are attacking my house! They want my dog!"

Pleakley tried to stop Jumba and Stitch from fighting, but they wouldn't listen to him. Pleakley grabbed Lilo and ran out of the house—just as Jumba and Stitch blew it to bits! KABOOM!

Nani arrived just in time to see Cobra Bubbles putting Lilo in his car. While Nani argued with Cobra, Lilo ran away into the woods.

When they saw she was gone, Cobra and Nani ran to find her.

Meanwhile, Stitch found Lilo. He pulled out his antennae and extra legs to show Lilo that he was an alien.

"You ruined everything!" Lilo cried. "Get out of here, Stitch!"

Suddenly, Captain Gantu appeared. The Grand Councilwoman had sent him to Earth to capture Stitch. He tossed a net over Stitch—*and* Lilo! Nani, who had just arrived, tried to stop him.

Stitch managed to escape. He tried to save Lilo, but it was too late. Gantu's spaceship took off with Lilo trapped inside!

At last Nani caught up to Stitch. "Where's Lilo?" she demanded.

As Stitch began to explain, Jumba jumped out of the bushes and grabbed him.

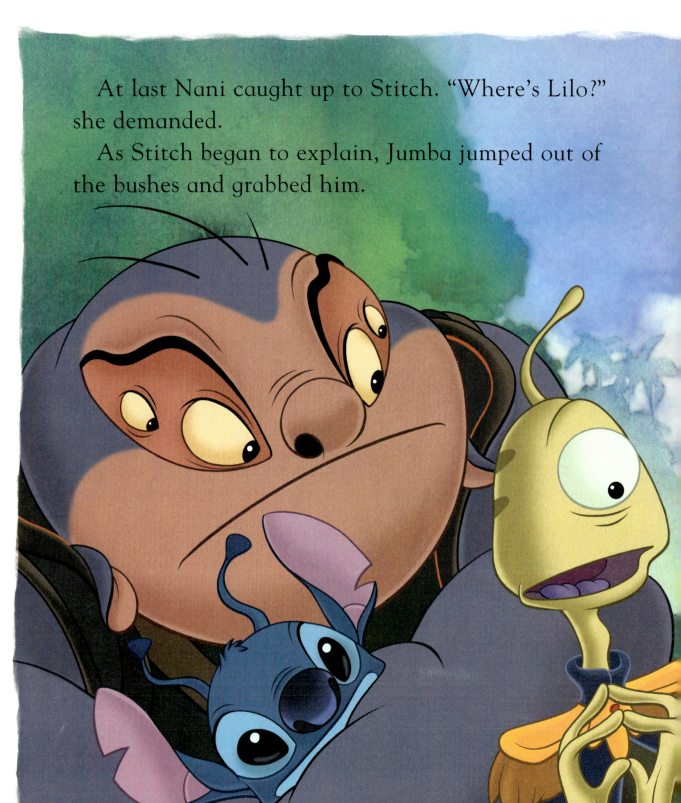

Pleakley pulled out his intergalactic communicator and called the Grand Councilwoman. "Experiment 626 is in custody," he said.

Nani stared at the aliens in amazement. "Wh-where's Lilo?" she cried again.

Nani thought her sister was gone forever. Jumba, Pleakley, and Stitch started to walk away. Stitch suddenly stopped and walked back to Nani.

"'Ohana means family," he said. "Family means . . ."

". . . nobody gets left behind," Nani finished.

Stitch convinced Jumba and Pleakley to release him. They had to rescue Lilo!

Jumba took the friends to the place where he had
hidden his spaceship when he first came to Earth.
They climbed aboard and flew after Gantu's ship.

"How did you get out?" Gantu shouted when he saw
Stitch at the ship's controls. He fired his lasers and
chased the spaceship.

Stitch jumped out of Jumba's ship to try to rescue
Lilo, but he fell down, down, down toward the ground.

"What do we do?" Nani asked.

"Hope for a miracle," Jumba replied. "That's all we *can* do."

Captain Gantu's ship raced downward and flew right past Stitch. "Don't leave me, okay?" Lilo cried.

Stitch heard Lilo and quickly developed a plan. He blasted himself up to Gantu's ship, rescued Lilo, and took her back to Jumba's spaceship.

Jumba's ship landed in the ocean. David was surfing nearby.

"Can you give us a ride to shore?" Lilo called.

David was a little confused at the sight of the aliens, but he nodded. "Sure," he said. "But I'll have to make two trips."

The Grand Councilwoman was waiting on the beach. "Take him to my ship," she commanded. Her guard moved toward Stitch.

Stitch hugged Lilo. "This is my family," he said.

Then Cobra reminded Lilo that she had the adoption papers from the animal shelter. "If you take him, you're stealing!" Lilo told the councilwoman.

The councilwoman realized Lilo was right. "This creature has been sentenced to life in exile," she announced, "on Earth."

Stitch was happy to stay. Lilo was happy to keep him. Nani was happy because Cobra Bubbles agreed that she and Lilo should remain together. Even Jumba and Pleakley were happy. The Grand Councilwoman left them behind on Earth, and they got to stay with Lilo and Nani, too.

They were one big out-of-this-world family!